What Will FAT CAT Sit On?

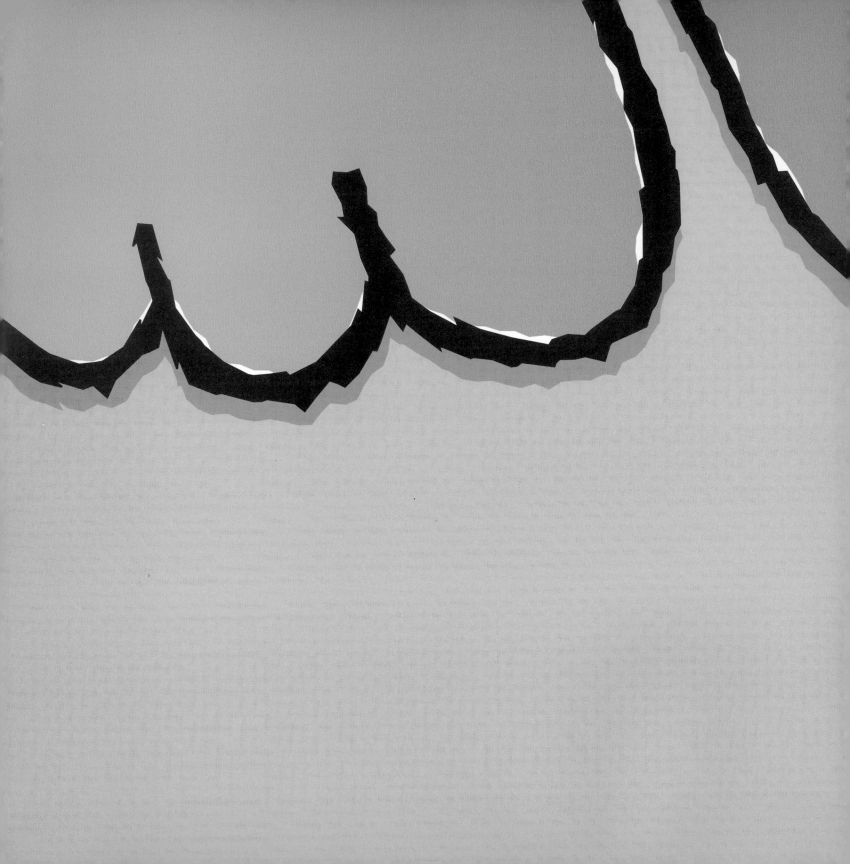

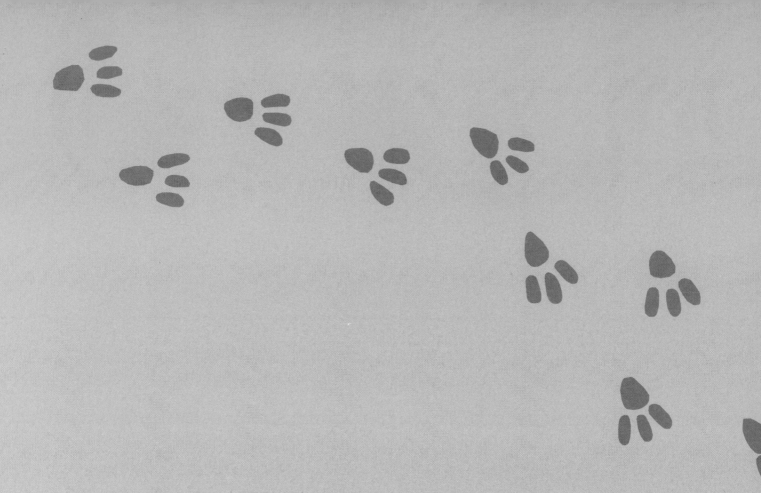

SCHOLASTIC INC.

New York Toronto London Auckland Sydney
Mexico City New Delhi Hong Kong Buenos Aires

Jan Thomas

What Will FAT CAT Sit On?

For Sam!

Will Fat Cat sit on...

NO!

Fat Cat will not sit on the

COW!

Will Fat Cat sit on...

the **CHICKEN**?

NO!

Fat Cat will not sit on the

CHICKEN

(or the pig).

NO!

Fat Cat will not sit on the

DOG!

OKAY, so Fat Cat will

NOT

sit on the cow,
or the chicken,
or the pig,
or the dog.

Then, what
WILL
Fat Cat sit on?

eeep?

Perhaps he could sit on the CHAIR?

The CHAIR!

Of

COURSE!

NOW,
what will Fat Cat ...

have for
LUNCH?

ISBN-13: 978-0-545-06697-6
ISBN-10: 0-545-06697-2

Copyright © 2007 by Jan Thomas.
All rights reserved. Published by Scholastic Inc.,
557 Broadway, New York, NY 10012, by arrangement with Harcourt, Inc.
SCHOLASTIC and associated logos are trademarks and/or
registered trademarks of Scholastic Inc.

12 11 10 9 8 7 6 5 4 3 2   8 9 10 11 12 13/0

Printed in the U.S.A.   40

First Scholastic printing, January 2008

The display and text types were set
in Eatwell Chubby and Chaloops.
Interior design by Lauren Rille
Cover design by Michele Wetherbee